IRISH LEGENDS FOR THE VERY YOUNG

NIAMH SHARKEY

MERCIER PRESS

For Don and Pat

First published in 1996 by
MERCIER PRESS
PO Box 5, 5 French Church Street,
Cork
Tel: (021) 275040; Fax: (021) 274969
e.mail: books@mercier.ie
16 Hume Street, Dublin 2
Tel: (01) 661 5299; Fax (01) 661 8583
e.mail: books@marino.ie

Trade enquiries to CMD DISTRIBUTION,
55a Spruce Avenue,
Stillorgan Industrial Park,
Blackrock, County Dublin
Tel: (01) 294 2560; Fax: (01) 294 2564

© Niamh Sharkey 1996
illustrations and text

ISBN 1 85635 144 0
10 9 8 7 6 5 4 3

A CIP record for this title is available
from the British Library

Cover illustration and design by Niamh
Sharkey
Set by Richard Parfrey
Printed in Ireland by Colour Books,
Baldoyle Industrial Estate, Dublin 13

CONTENTS

HOW SETANTA BECAME CÚCHULAINN

When little Setanta went to sleep at night, he dreamed wonderful dreams.

In these dreams he was a Red Branch knight with a silver sword and a golden shield. He was the bravest warrior in all Ireland and could fight any man or beast.

Charging through dark woods on horse-back, riding through the deepest of glens or climbing the highest mountains, Setanta would have fantastic adventures. But all dreams must come to an end and in the morning when he awoke, Setanta was still just a boy.

During the sunny days, Setanta loved

to go hunting and fishing with his father. His father's name was Sualtaim; he was a brave warrior and taught Setanta many things.

The two would set off in the darkness before sunrise and go hunting in the forests near their home. Sualtaim brought his son everywhere, teaching him the ways of a warrior.

For his seventh birthday, Setanta got a hurley stick and a tiny silver ball from his father and mother. Setanta thought his presents were marvellous and he played with them all day. He even brought them to bed with him!

Setanta asked his father every day, 'When will I be old enough to join the Red Branch knights?'

Sualtaim would answer: 'Setanta, you're only seven years old. The Red Branch knights are all fully grown men. Maybe next year I'll let you join the Machra.'

The Machra were like boy scouts, young boys who learned the skills of hunting and sport. They trained to be young

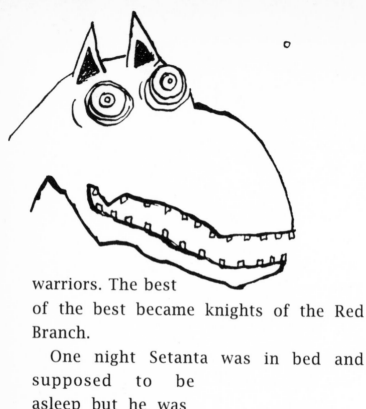

warriors. The best
of the best became knights of the Red
Branch.

One night Setanta was in bed and
supposed to be
asleep but he was
awake and feeling

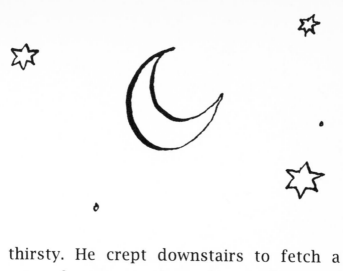

thirsty. He crept downstairs to fetch a
cup of water and as he reached the
kitchen door he heard his mother and
father talking.

He put his ear to the
door and realised that
they were talking

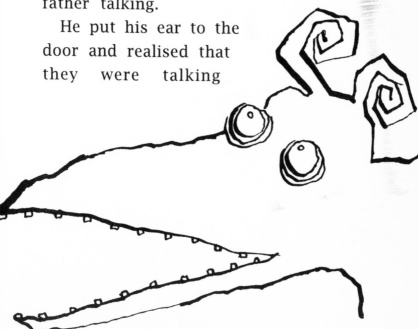

about his mother's brother Conor, who lived at Emhain Macha. His uncle was the king of Ulster! The Red Branch knights lived in his castle!

Setanta could not believe his ears. He decided there and then to travel to his uncle's stronghold, sure that the king would let him join the knights of the Red Branch.

Setanta crept upstairs, dressed himself for a journey and took up his hurley and silver ball. He tiptoed past the kitchen and let himself out the front door.

It was pitch dark outside when he started and the journey was a slow one. During the day he threw his silver ball high in the air as he walked, and bounced it along with his stick. At night he slept under the stars in the dark forests.

His sleep was light since he knew the woods were full of wild animals who might gobble him up for dinner.

After many days like this Setanta at last reached his uncle's great fort. Outside, a group of boys were playing hurling.

They were the older boys from the Machra.
Setanta jumped in and started to play,
even though he was tired from his long
journey. He ran rings around the older
boys, even slipping under a taller boy's
legs to score a goal.

He shouted in delight but when he
turned around, ten sets of angry eyes
stared at him. The Machra were very very
upset to be beaten by such a small fellow.

The ten angry boys jumped on Setanta

but again he was more than fit for the lot of them. He tossed them to the ground and broke all their hurleys.

King Conor was looking from his bed-

room window in the castle and was amazed to see ten of his best young warriors beaten by such a small boy. He hurried outside to talk to him.

Conor called to the boy: 'Who are you?' Setanta turned around. 'My name is Setanta,' he said, 'son of Dechtire and Sualtaim. I have travelled many miles to join the company of the Red Branch knights.'

'My goodness,' cried the king, 'you are my sister's child. I am your uncle, Conor the king. Welcome to Emhain Macha.

'As to your wish to join the Red Branch...' The king shook his head. 'I'm sorry, nephew, but you are far too young. All the knights are fully grown men. Maybe in a couple of years you will have a better chance.'

Setanta was sad. His dreams were shattered. When Conor saw the tears in Setanta's eyes he had an idea. 'Why don't you explore the fort and then follow me to Culann's castle. He is throwing a feast and all the Red Branch knights will be there. You will meet them.'

King Conor's castle was huge. Setanta counted one hundred and fifty rooms! The ceilings were made of copper and bronze that sparkled like gold. Setanta could see his reflection in them as he ran about.

As the sun began to sink Setanta began

the long trek to Culann's castle. He was so excited: at last he was to meet the Red Branch knights!

Culann was the most famous smith in Ulster. Smiths forged weapons for the warriors and Culann made the deadliest swords. If your finger even touched the blade of one of his weapons it would bleed. Culann was throwing a mighty feast to follow a day of hunting on his lands. It was to thank Conor and his knights for buying their swords from him.

The feasters were entertained by feats of juggling, poetry, songs and dancing. There was plenty of food and too much wine. Towards the end of the feast Culann turned to Conor to ask, 'Is anyone else coming to the feast?'

Conor was more than a little drunk; he had had too much red wine. Culann was a blur in front of him. Conor forgot that he had asked little Setanta to come along later. 'No, I don't think so,' he answered. 'Why?'

Culann replied that he had a great

The feasters were enter-tained by feats of juggling, poetry, songs and dancing. There was plenty of food and too much wine....

TOO MUCH WINE

hound tied up in the grounds.

'He is the most feared dog in Ireland, with the strength of one hundred men. If nobody else is coming I will set him free to protect us while we're sleeping.'

'That's fine by me,' said King Conor as he stumbled up-stairs to bed.

A great yellow moon glowed in the purple sky above Setanta's head as he made his way to Culann's fort. The night was so cold he could see his breath making patterns in the air.

Ahead of him he could just make out the soft glow of Culann's castle in the distance. He decided to sit down for a little rest.

A bloodcurdling howl made him freeze.

HOWL

HOWL

HOWL

A   second
howl echoed through the
forest. He stood up, trying not to
make a sound. He couldn't see anything
moving at all.

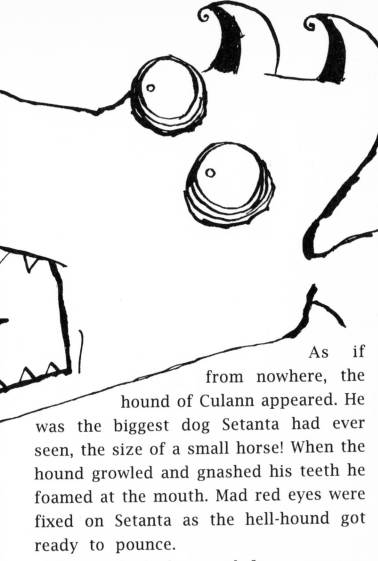

As if from nowhere, the hound of Culann appeared. He was the biggest dog Setanta had ever seen, the size of a small horse! When the hound growled and gnashed his teeth he foamed at the mouth. Mad red eyes were fixed on Setanta as the hell-hound got ready to pounce.

Setanta looked around for a weapon. Tossing sods of grass at this barking mad dog wouldn't save him; his hurley and ball were his only chance.

Suddenly the hound leapt, and as it did so Setanta took a deep breath, bounced his silver ball on the ground and smacked it with his hurley. With the speed of light the silver ball flew through the air and got the hound right between the eyes! The beast stopped in mid-flight and fell to the ground at the boy's feet.

King Conor fell across the bed, asleep before he even had time to cover himself with his bearskin. He awoke almost immediately to the sound of chilling howls and the noise of fighting.

He dashed from the bedroom and ran down the steps of the castle shouting, 'I forgot about little Setanta. He will be minced up by the hound of Culann.'

Half-dressed Red Branch knights ran out into the dark, followed by Culann and Conor. The sight that met them made them rub their eyes: they found a little boy standing beside the dead hound.

Culann cried in horror, 'What has happened to my mastiff?'

'I am truly sorry,' said the boy. 'I am Setanta, son of Sualtaim. I am the one who killed your guard dog with my silver ball.'

'I am glad that you are safe, young Setanta,' said Culann sadly, 'but I shall be lost without my hound that I loved and that protected me when I went to sleep at night.'

'Do not worry, Culann,' said Setanta in a manly voice. 'I shall find you the cleverest whelp in the country and train it to be the best watchdog in Ireland. Until that day *I* will guard your sheep and your castle against invaders.'

Culann scratched his head and then smiled broadly. 'Thank you, Setanta,' he said. 'I am content that you shall guard my castle for you have proved that you are stronger than any hound. Henceforth your name will be Cú Chulainn, "Culann's hound".'

The Red Branch knights laughed when

they heard that a seven-year-old boy was to be the new hound of Culann.

Setanta was delighted to meet the knights at last. He went around shaking all their hands and asking their names. He had to tell them crossly to stop laughing: he was going to be the best guard dog on two legs that they had ever seen.

Cúchulainn became the best guard in the whole of Ireland. The smith made him a special sword and shield to guard

his fort. When the Red Branch knights saw how strong he was they asked him to join, even though he was still a young boy. Setanta's dream had come true!

Even when Cúchulainn became the leader and the most famous of the Red Branch knights, he always kept the little silver ball close at hand. It had once saved his life, and there was no way of knowing when he would need it again.

THE
CHILDREN
OF LIR

T he children
took a deep
breath and dived
underneath the
amber waves of
Lake Derravaragh,
tumbling down-
wards past
dancing weeds.

Fionnuala opened her eyes to look for Aodh, her brother, and saw him sitting on a rock with a circle of fish swimming about his head. Fionnuala swam over and frightened them all away.

She and Aodh were no ordinary children. They had gills behind their ears and webbed fingers and toes. They were the children of Lir, happiest under the water, where the fish welcomed them as friends.

When they came up for air, they saw their father by the shore. Lir stood taller than most of his tribe, the Tuatha dé Danann. Lir was Lord of the Sea. His eyes were the green-blue of tidal pools. His hair looked like seaweed, all knotty.

Lir was sad. The children ran over to him, to find out why he was so sad. The three sat down by the lake.

'I'm afraid that I have some bad news,' he said. 'Your mother has died giving birth to twin boys. They will be called Fiachra and Conn. I hope you will help me to look after them.' Lir took his children by the hand. 'Let's go home,' he said.

Home was the White Fort. Lir and his
children walked up the pathway made
from shells. Fionnuala felt like crying but
she had to be brave.

When they got home she went up to
her room, which was painted in twenty

shades of blue. She lay down on her bed and looked at the ceiling, where little starfish and sea horses swam. The room looked like a cave under the sea. It made her feel safe. Fionnuala missed her mother already but she made a promise that she would look after her brothers.

After Aebh, the mother, died, Fionnuala tried to look after the fort. It was so big that she spent half her time housekeeping. The rest was spent running after Fiachra and Conn. They were little rascals, climbing up trees, gobbling the apples. Sometimes they put handfuls of spiders and worms in Fionnuala's bed. Mostly the children of Lir were friends and when Fiachra and Conn were old enough, they all went swimming in the lake together.

Their father did not

want to play with the children. Instead, he went hunting with his warriors, often not returning for days.

Bodb Derg was the King of Connacht. He was the children's grandfather. His castle was by Lough Derg, on the Shannon. Once when Lir returned from his travels, he took his children to visit their grandfather.

Bodb Derg was as tall as Lir, with fiery red hair and a big bushy beard. He loved the children of Lir with all his heart. Little Fiachra and Conn were a bit afraid of his size but when he swirled them in the air, they giggled.

They played with Aoife, who was their mother's sister.

When Aoife was there Lir forgot his sadness and started to smile again. She was beautiful, the image of their mother.

The children were happy that their father was smiling again and many days were spent swimming in the lake, fishing or having feasts in the forest. A short time later Lir asked Aoife to be his wife. She said yes. They were to be a family again.

The wedding was held deep in the forest. Afterwards, all the guests went back to the White Fort.

When the sun went down, a great fire was lit. Singers, dancers and musicians entertained the guests, who joined in the dancing round the fire. Little yellow stars glowed in the sky. The celebration went on till daybreak.

The year after the wedding was a happy one. The White Fort was painted and repaired. Aoife was like a mother to the children. Lir was happy. He played with his children, swimming in the lake or chasing them around the garden. He hated to go away hunting because he missed Fionnuala, Aodh, Fiachra and Conn so much.

After a year things began to change. Aoife could not have any children of her own. She became jealous when she saw Lir playing with the children.

One day, as Lir was playing with Fiachra and Conn, Fionnuala sat under a tree beside Aoife. Suddenly a scowl came across Aoife's face. Her green eyes went dark with hatred. She wanted a child of her own. Why should she look after her sister's children? She wanted Lir all to herself.

From that moment everything changed. Aoife no longer went on walks with Fionnuala. She no longer looked after the fort. Behind Lir's back she scolded the children and stopped them swimming in the lake or playing in the fields.

Sometimes Aoife's face looked so evil that Fiachra and Conn would burst into tears if she came near. Fionnuala feared that something would happen to her brothers. She remembered the promise she had made. One evening she overheard Aoife talking to Lir.

'Those children are no good. Fionnuala is lazy, Aodh has his head in the clouds, and as for the other two, well, they have just come into the fort, plastered in mud!'

Lir would hear nothing bad about his children. The more Aoife complained the less he listened. Aoife became so sick with jealousy that she went to bed for a year.

One morning when Lir was away, Aoife appeared at the door of the fort.

'Children,' she said with a wide smile, 'I'm feeling better. It's a lovely day to visit your grandfather. Aodh, could you fetch the chariot.'

Fionnuala felt a shiver go down her spine. The night before she had been warned in a dream not to go with Aoife. Yet it seemed silly now. What could she possibly do if the children where going to see Bodb Derg?

Fionnuala helped the cook to prepare food for the journey. Aodh got the chariot ready. Fiachra and Conn stayed quiet, afraid of Aoife, in case she shouted at them.

When they set out for Bodb Derg's castle, everything seemed like the old days. Aoife was smiling and telling the children stories about when she was a young girl.

The day was hot and they stopped by a small lake for their picnic. The children ran over to the lake. The water looked very inviting and Aoife called over, 'Why don't you go for a swim before lunch; it's such a lovely day.' Fionnuala thought: no harm can come to us in the water. So they all jumped in.

The lake was cold but the children splashed around laughing. Suddenly, they stopped and looked around for Aoife. She was standing by the shore, dressed in a black cloak with strange patterns on the sleeves, and with a look of hatred on her face. She had a long black stick in her right hand.

Fionnuala knew what it was. A druid stick, which was used for wicked spells! Fionnuala wished she had paid attention to her dream.

The children couldn't move. They were frozen to the spot. Aoife began waving the stick in the air and speaking in a strange voice:

Out with you upon the wild waves, children of the king! Henceforth your cries shall be with the flocks of the birds.

A white light glowed on the top of the
magic wand. Aoife pointed it at the
children of Lir. The white light darted
out of the wand across the water and the
children could not feel their
hands or feet. A strange tingling
ran through their bones.

Fionnuala looked around for
her brothers. She cried
in shock. Three
beautiful

white swans floated beside
her. Fionnuala looked
at her reflection.
A swan blinked
back at her.

'What spell have you cast on us?' Aodh cried.

Aoife laughed, 'I have changed you into the shape of swans. And so you will stay for nine hundred years. The spell will be broken only when a man from the north marries a woman from the south. Or when you hear the bells of a church ringing. I have also put you under a *geis*. That is a special spell which makes you do what I want you to do.'

'What do you mean?' asked Fiachra.

'By my spell,' cried the stepmother, 'I shall have you spend the first three

hundred years on the lake beside your home. Then you shall fly to the icy waters between Ireland and Scotland. The final years will be spent on the island of Inis Glora off the western coast.'

With that Aoife climbed into the chariot and sped off to her father's house. When she arrived at the fort she told the children's grandfather a terrible tale, that the children had been eaten by wild animals.

Lir was sent for. When he heard that his children had vanished, he went to look for them, setting off on his golden chariot. On the way to Bodb Derg's fort he heard singing. He stopped the chariot and followed the sound. There in the water four white swans were singing a sad tune.

'Father, we are your children. Aoife has changed us into swans for nine hundred years!' Lir was heartbroken. When he tried to lift one of the swans out of the water he failed. Aoife's spell made it impossible to move them from the lake.

Fiachra and Conn started to cry. They couldn't understand what was happening, since they were only six years old.

'Do not worry, children,' said their father, trying to be cheerful. 'I will build a house beside the lake. We can talk all day. First, I must tell your grandfather how wicked his daughter was.'

When
Bodb Derg
heard this
news his heart
was also broken.
Aoife grew afraid
because her father's
magic was stronger
than hers. With a wave
of his wand, he changed
Aoife into a demon with scaly skin and
a tongue pointed like an arrow. She flew

38

around Lir's head, shrieking loudly, and burst out the window, never to be seen again.

The years passed quickly. People came from all over Ireland to visit the children of Lir, stopping by the dwelling that Lir had built to be near his loved ones. They came to hear Fionnuala and her brothers sing.

One evening as Lir sat and talked to his children, he realised that they would soon have to leave. The swans looked as beautiful as ever but Lir had grown old. His hair was silvery-grey and his face was wrinkled. Lir was too sad to speak. Instead he kissed each swan on the head.

The next morning they took flight, circling the spot where their father stood, with eyes the colour of the sea. Tears ran down Lir's cheeks as he wept for the children he would never see again.

The years that the children of Lir spent on Lake Derravaragh had been happy ones. They had friends around them and their father by their side. Now they had to leave the lake waters and they hated it. As they flew on their journey to the northern sea they looked down at the castles and fields of green far below them.

The waters of their new home were icy-cold and the bewitched children had no friends. No one heard their beautiful singing except the fish and the seagulls. They stayed close, hugging each other to keep warm.

This cold sea was to be their home for the next three hundred years and it was no wonder that they were always hungry and sad. During the winter the sea froze. Their feathers would stick to the ice. Fionnuala would spread her wings and try to keep her brothers warm.

Though they knew day from night and could tell when summer ended and winter began, they could not count the years. Yet one morning the children knew it was time to leave. They could not believe that they had spent six hundred years as swans! Fionnuala was looking forward to flying back to the west of Ireland, to see her home.

On the way, they saw that Ireland had changed. The swans flew over their old home, the White Fort, but it was only a ruin; nettles grew where the doorway used to be. The Tuatha dé Danann were long gone. Fionnuala tried to explain to her brothers that their father was dead.

The children flew on to Inis Glora and stayed for another three hundred years. After an age-long time an old man came to live on the island. He was the first human that the children had seen for years and they longed to talk to him. One day, the old man was washing his clothes in the lake. He smiled at the four swans. 'How are you beauties doing?' he asked. 'Would you like some bread?'

'That would be lovely,' replied Fionnuala. The old man fell backwards and landed with his bottom

Did one of you speak

in the water. 'Did one of you speak?' he asked in disbelief.

'We are the children of Lir. My name is Fionnuala and these are my brothers Aodh, Conn and Fiachra,' Fionnuala said, as she paddled over to the man.

'I thought the story of the children of Lir was only make-believe.' he said. 'I am a holy man, sent here to build a church.'

Fionnuala was delighted when she heard this. When Aoife made the spell she said it would be broken only if the children heard the bell of a church ringing or when a man from the north was to marry a woman from the south. Fionnuala could see the end coming near.

Many warriors from Connacht came to the holy man to give him old swords and spears. These were to be melted down to make a bell. The news made the children of Lir very excited. They swam on the lake, singing songs with their lovely voices.

On the day the bell was ready, a warrior arrived to steal the swans. He was Lairgain, King of Connacht. He had promised the singing swans to his new wife, the princess of Munster. The princess had heard stories of their beautiful voices and wanted them for the pond in her garden.

The holy man tried to fight Lairgain off but he was too weak. The king put Fionnuala and her brothers in his chariot. They flapped their wings and shrieked. 'Set us free; we are the children of Lir!'

At that moment the swans heard the bell ringing, loud, dingle-dangling. It was music to their ears. Fionnuala then knew the spell was broken. The king cried out in

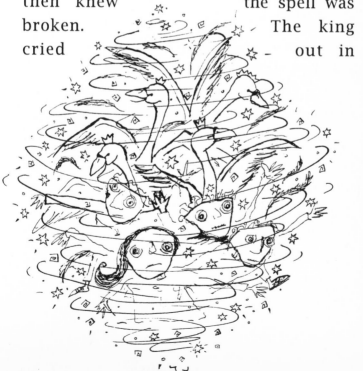

horror as the swans in front of him changed. White feathers fell and swirled in the air. The swans were gone, and standing in front of the king were four old people. But their eyes sparkled.

The children of Lir had been waiting nine hundred years and now the spell was broken. Fionnuala hugged her three brothers in delight.

They spent the rest of their days with the holy man, telling him stories of the evil Aoife and how she had been changed into a demon. They also told of their sad days spent on the frozen sea, fighting the waves. Although their tale was a mournful one, for the rest of their days they were happy.

Fionnuala and her three brothers liked to sit by the lake in the evenings and as they watched the golden stars appear they remembered their father playing jockey-back with Fiachra and Conn or swimming underneath the water with Fionnuala and Aodh.

They
sometimes stayed up
all night recalling the White
Fort and the fun they had as the children
of Lir. And strangely, as they talked, the
nine hundred years seemed as short as
a single day.

OISÍN IN
TÍR NA nÓG

T ír na nÓg lies over the blue waves, further than the eye can see. In that magic land you never grow old. Time stands still, there is plenty of honey and wine, the trees always have leaves and your hair never turns white. You live for ever and ever. It never rains or snows and the wind is no more than a cooling breeze.

Oisín was the son of Finn, the leader of the Fianna. His name meant 'little fawn' and he was a poet as well as a warrior. Sometimes his poems were so long that it took him a whole day to recite them. He had a mop of red curly hair and sparkling eyes the colour of acorns.

One summer's day, the Fianna had stopped by the shores of one of the lakes of Killarney to have their midday feast. Oisín was playing with the dogs, making up some funny poems about how many times a dog wags his tail in one day! All the Fianna were laughing at Oisín's poems when a strange thing happened: a white mist appeared and surrounded them.

Out of the mist a girl appeared, riding a horse as white as snow. Golden hair hung in ringlets down her back. She wore a dress that had patterns of the moon and the stars painted on it. Her eyes were blue with a golden fleck and she was clearly not of this world, for even her white horse had a golden saddle that was decorated with tiny starfish. The warriors were silent; they had never seen a woman so beautiful.

Oisín's father Finn showed no fear. 'Tell me your name, fair princess, and where you come from,' he said.

'I am Niamh of the Golden Hair, I come from Tír na nÓg to meet your son Oisín,' she said, and Oisín thought her voice sounded lovely. 'I have travelled over the waves to meet

him, for I have heard of his beautiful poems and songs. Is he here?'

Oisín stepped forward. When Niamh saw his curly red locks and dancing eyes she fell in love. 'If you wish I will follow you to the end of the world,' he said.

The fairy maiden began to tell him about her enchanted land where all his wishes would be granted. 'It's a wonderful place. The sun never sets, rain never falls and you shall never grow old. Time stands still in Tír na nÓg; a year will pass by like a day. You will have a hundred swords, a hundred horses and a hundred warriors. In fact, you may have a hundred of whatever you wish.'

As Niamh was telling Oisín about Tír na nÓg his eyes got bigger and bigger. Finn saw the effect of her words and was worried, for he knew that if Oisín went to Tír na nÓg he would never return. Nobody had ever returned from there.

Oisín turned to his father. 'Do not worry,' he said. 'If I go with Niamh I will return in a short while.' His father had no choice but to let him go with her.

As if in a dream, Oisín mounted the white horse behind Niamh and waved goodbye to his father and the rest of the Fianna. The white horse neighed three times and galloped towards the mountains. Finn was sad when he heard no sound coming from the hoofbeats of the white horse. He knew it was the last time that he would see his son.

The horse ran as fast as the wind over hills and through forests. When they reached the sea, it snorted twice and dashed into the surf. The sea swirled around the horse's hooves, splashing Niamh and Oisín, who were sitting on the saddle.

Oisín could see a storm approaching. Black clouds opened, spilling rain over the sea. Lightning flashed and thunder rolled but the white horse never faltered. After some time the rain stopped and the sun came out, drying their clothes and making them warm again.

On their way to Tír na nÓg they passed a barren grey island in the middle of the

ocean. 'Where are we, Niamh?' asked Oisín.

'At the home of Fomór of the Mighty Blows,' said Niamh. 'He is a cruel giant and he keeps a young princess a prisoner in his tower. No man has ever dared to rescue her.' Now Oisín was firstly a warrior and when he heard

about the poor princess he asked Niamh to take him to the island.

When they reached the path that led to the giant's castle Oisín took out his silver sword and held it in front of him. As he reached the dark castle he pounded with his fist on the heavy door.

WHO'S THAT KNOCKING AT MY door?

thundered a booming voice that made Oisín's legs wobble.

'I am Oisín, son of Finn,' he replied.
The door creaked open and when Oisín
saw the owner of the castle he could
hardly believe his eyes. The giant was a

terrifying sight, big and ugly, with a mop of wild black hair that hid his horrible face. The remains of his dinner hung from his scraggy beard. Oisín nearly fainted from the foul smell of his breath. The giant raised a club covered with spikes and the fight began.

It lasted for three days and three nights. Oisín spent most of his time ducking and weaving so that the giant would not hit him with the spiky club. At the end of the three days, the giant was exhausted from running after Oisín. He stopped to catch his breath and Oisín, seeing his chance, cut the giant's head off with one mighty stroke.

The fight was over and Oisín rushed into the castle to set the princess free. She was the happiest person in the world and she could not thank Niamh and Oisín enough for saving her from the wicked giant Fomór.

The next morning Niamh and Oisín headed off on the second half of their journey to Tír na nÓg. After a long day, they saw a speck of land in the distance.

As they came closer Oisín saw an island with rolling green hills and a gleaming white castle standing on a cliff overlooking the sea. It was a sight to feast the eyes on. The white horse shook the water off his coat as he trotted up the beach. Small clusters of seaweed were stuck to his hoofs but he didn't seem to mind. They were home.

'Welcome to Tír na nÓg,' said Niamh, and she kissed Oisín on the lips. The king and queen came down to the beach to welcome them. A hundred warriors and maidens welcomed them also.

Oisín looked around this wonderful place. All the houses were decorated with shells and jewels of sparkling colours. Apple, orange and lemon trees grew in the gardens.

A welcoming party was held in the white castle. The guests ate from silver plates, with golden knives and forks. The feast went on for ten days and ten nights with singing, dancing and feasting. At the end of the ten days, Niamh and Oisín were married under an orange tree as the sun went down.

Tír na nÓg was everything that Niamh had promised and more. The sun shone every day, Oisín ate the best food and listened to beautiful music and he was very happy to be with Niamh. Yet he missed his father and his fellow warriors of the Fianna. He longed to return to

Ireland to tell them how happy he was.

Oisín felt he had been in Tír na nÓg for only a short while. He forgot that time did not exist there. A year passed by like an hour. When he talked to Niamh about returning to Ireland he was shocked to hear he had been away for over three hundred years.

Niamh was afraid to let Oisín go in case he might not return but she knew that if he didn't see Ireland again he would always be a little sad. 'I will let you go,' said Niamh, 'if you promise not to get down off the white horse. If you do you can never return to Tír na nÓg.'

Oisín promised Niamh that he would stay in the saddle. When Niamh kissed Oisín goodbye, she felt in her heart that she would never see her husband again. He climbed into the saddle of the white horse and galloped towards the waves.

When he reached the shores of Ireland, Oisín was shocked to see that everything had changed. The men and women looked like dwarfs, they were so small! Oisín was the size of a giant compared to these little people.

He rode wildly around Ireland on his white horse, searching for Finn and the Fianna. But no matter where he went there was no sign of his father or his old comrades. He decided to go home but when he got there, he saw his father's fortress lying in ruins, overgrown with nettles and brambles. The scene made him very sad. In the field beside his broken-down home Oisín saw a group of men. He rode over to them and asked, 'What has happened to Finn and the Fianna?'

The men were amazed at the size of Oisín. 'Finn died a long time ago,' said one of them. 'He had a son called Oisín who rode away with a beautiful woman on a fairy horse. But that was hundreds of years ago.'

Oisín was too sad to tell the men that he was Oisín, son of Finn; so he turned his fairy white horse towards the west, and galloped away with tears in his eyes.

On his way to the sea, he passed by Glen na Smole where he used to go hunting with the Fianna. Oisín remembered happy times spent here.

Down in the valley a group of men were trying to lift a large stone that one of the Fianna could have lifted with one hand. It was a sorry sight. When Oisín came closer one of the men asked, 'Gentle giant, will you help us move this stone?'

Feeling sorry for the men, Oisín said he would gladly help. Remembering Niamh's words, he did not get down from

the horse. Instead, he leaned forward, grabbed the stone and hurled it away. The men gasped at his strength.

But alas, as Oisín threw the stone away, the golden stirrup snapped and Oisín fell to the ground! The white horse neighed loudly, shook his head and sped away over the mountain.

Oisín started to change. He felt weak and his arms and legs began to tingle and lose all their strength. His curly red locks turned white and his face became wrinkled. The men couldn't believe their eyes!

A beautiful friendly giant had turned into a wizened old man

before their very eyes!

A frail voice said, 'I am Oisín, son of Finn. I have returned from Tír na nÓg after three hundred years. My wife Niamh, warned me not   to get down off the white horse. Now I under-stand   why. I shall never see my love again.'

Over the waves, in the magical land of Tír na nÓg the white horse ran towards the castle. When Niamh saw that the golden saddle was empty, she cried for her lost Oisín who would never return to her again.